EXPLORING THE UNIVERSE

The NIGHT SKY

ROBIN KERROD

RSVP
RAINTREE
STECK-VAUGHN
PUBLISHERS

A Harcourt Company

Austin   New York
www.raintreesteckvaughn.com

**First American edition published in 2002
by Raintree Steck-Vaughn Publishers**

© 2002 by Graham Beehag Books

Raintree Steck-Vaughn Publishers
4515 Seton Center Parkway
Austin, Texas 78755

Website address: www.raintreesteckvaughn.com

Library of Congress Cataloging-in-Publication Data

Kerrod, Robin.
   Exploring the night sky / Robin Kerrod.
      p. cm. — (Exploring the universe)
   Includes bibliographical references and index.
   Summary: Explores astronomy, discussing both ancient research and modern developments.
   ISBN 0-7398-2815-0
   1. Astronomy—Juvenile literature. [1. Astronomy.]

QB46 .K417 2001
520—dc21   2001031674

Printed and bound in the United States.

1 2 3 4 5 6 7 8 9 0 05 04 03 02 01

Contents

Introduction

In this book we explore the fascinating world of astronomy—the scientific study of the heavens. Astronomy began with the earliest humans to look in the night sky at the stars and wonder about what they saw there. With the first great civilizations of the Middle East and elsewhere, astronomy became a subject of scientific and religious study.

Like our early ancestors, we begin our study of astronomy with simple stargazing, using only our eyes to observe what happens in the heavens. We will learn how to recognize the constellations, those glittering patterns of bright stars in which our ancestors saw shapes and meaning. In Section Three of the book, a set of star maps is included so that you can identify the constellations as they appear in the night sky in the different seasons.

Stargazing with only our eyes gives just a hint of what the universe of stars, planets, and galaxies is like. Looking at the heavens through binoculars or a telescope brings more spectacular sights into view, delighting the eye and exciting the imagination—sights such as colorful clouds of glowing gas, and clusters of stars sparkling like jewels.

The Hubble Space Telescope captured this beautiful image of Galaxy NGC 4214. Located some 13 million light-years from Earth, NGC 4214 is currently forming clusters of new stars from its interstellar gas and dust.

From lofty mountaintop observatories, today's astronomers peer at the distant heavens with giant telescopes, able to spy objects whose light has been traveling towards Earth from unimaginable distances for billions of years.

Even stranger sights are viewed by space telescopes such as the Hubble—newborn stars and planetary systems, dying suns blasting themselves apart. Nearer home, unmanned probes explore our own planetary system—spying volcanoes erupting on Jupiter's moon, Io, finding evidence of flowing water on Mars.

Though astronomy is one of the oldest sciences, there is nothing old-fashioned about the way astronomy is practiced today. Practically every day brings some new insight from today's astronomers about the way the universe began and how it works.

THE DAWN OF ASTRONOMY

The beginnings of astronomy can be traced back more than 5000 years, to the very beginnings of civilization. Until only about 400 years ago, astronomy had to rely only on observations that could be made with the eye alone. Then the invention of the telescope opened up a new window on the universe.

In all likelihood, prehistoric people looked at the night sky and marveled at its beauty. Humans probably did not start studying the heavens carefully until about 10,000 years ago, when they began farming and living a more settled life. They may have used their observations of the night sky to determine such things as the change of seasons and when was the right time to sow crops. The oldest known astronomical records date to about 3000 BC, when writing developed in the Middle East.

There, the Babylonians recorded astronomical observations on clay tablets in cuneiform writing (a system of writing with wedge-shaped marks pressed into soft clay, or cut into stone). The Egyptians kept records in the form of hieroglyphics, or picture writing. These early records show that, in the Middle East at least, astronomy was already well advanced.

The Egyptians worked out an accurate calendar, based on a year of 365 days, much like the one we use today. The ancient Chinese developed an accurate calendar, too. They also noted unusual events in the heavens—they recorded eclipses as far back as 4000 BC.

The prehistoric people in Europe must have had some knowledge of astronomy, too. They built huge stone circles, such as Stonehenge in England, which dates from about 2000 BC. Stonehenge seems to have been a kind of observatory. Its huge stones, or megaliths, seem to have been laid out with a specific purpose in mind. Certain stones lined up at certain times of the year to point to where, for example, the Sun rose on the summer solstice—the longest day of the year.

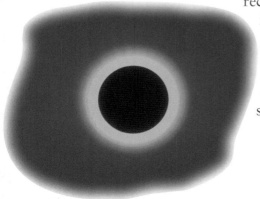

Left: Total eclipses of the Sun scared ancient peoples. But as early as 585 BC, the Greek astronomer Thales was able to predict when eclipses would occur.

The ancient Egyptians laid out the great
pyramids with great precision, aligning them
with prominent stars.

The ancient observatory Stonehenge as it is today. It is located near the town of Amesbury on Salisbury Plain, England. The most striking features are the trilithons, tall structures built of two massive sandstone blocks with another block on top.

Greek Astronomy

The civilization developed by the ancient Egyptians along the Nile River thrived for more than 2,000 years. Weakened by internal squabbles, it was invaded and occupied by a succession of foreign powers, beginning in about 945 BC. By then another powerful civilization was flourishing in the Mediterranean—ancient Greece.

The ancient Greeks built on the knowledge of the heavens inherited from the Babylonians and Egyptians. From 600 BC, Greek philosophers began trying to understand what happened in the heavens and how the universe worked. They laid the foundations for scientific astronomy.

The Egyptians had believed in a flat Earth, but Greek philosophers such as Aristotle (fourth century BC) thought otherwise. The Earth had to be round, they argued. As evidence, they pointed out that the shadow of the Earth on the Moon during an eclipse of the Moon was curved.

The Fixed Earth
Aristotle taught that the round Earth was fixed at the center of the universe and that the Sun, Moon, and planets circled around it.

About a century after Aristotle, Aristarchus determined that the motions of the heavenly bodies could just as easily be explained if Earth was a planet and circled around the Sun. Aristarchus was right, of course, but his ideas were too far ahead of their time.

The Great Observer
The greatest Greek observational astronomer was undoubtedly Hipparchus, who lived in the second century BC. He

Right: The universe according to Ptolemy. Earth is in the center, with the moon (Luna), Sun (Solis), and planets circling around it.

Below: Ptolemy introduced the idea of deferents and epicycles to explain the peculiar movement of the planets in the sky. Each planet, he said, moved in a circle (epicycle) around a point that moved in a circle (deferent) around Earth.

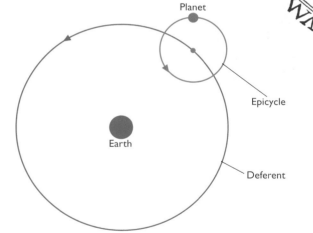

Ptolemy's View

Hipparchus's work would have been lost were it not for the last great Greek astronomer, Ptolemy of Alexandria, who lived in the 2nd century AD. He included it in a book he wrote that summed up all the astronomical and scientific knowledge of the time. His book has survived in an Arab translation and is usually called the *Almagest.*

Ptolemy set out the accepted view of the universe—a spherical Earth, around which the heavenly bodies traveled in circles. The stars were fixed to the inside of a great celestial (heavenly) sphere surrounding Earth. This Earth-centered view of the universe is known as the Ptolemaic system.

drew up a catalog charting the position and brightness of almost 1000 stars. He devised the magnitude system by which astronomers still classify star brightness: the brightest stars we can see are of the first magnitude, and the faintest stars are of the sixth magnitude; other stars have magnitudes in between.

In the East

Much of the knowledge obtained by the ancient Greeks was passed on to the Roman Empire, which at its peak stretched over much of Europe, North Africa, and the Middle East. In the 5th century, the empire fell into decline and came under attack from barbarian tribes.

With the fall of Rome, a period known as the Dark Ages began in Europe. Interest in learning and science—including astronomy—declined, and much earlier knowledge was lost and forgotten.

During this time, however, astronomers in other parts of the world were making advances. In the east, in India, astronomers were building primitive observatories. Arab astronomers were building new instruments, such as the astrolabe, to measure the positions of stars. By the 9th century, the city of Baghdad (in what is now Iraq) was the site of the finest observatory the world had ever known.

Above: An Arabian astrolabe, used to measure the angles of stars above the horizon. An astronomer trained the sighting bar on a star, then read the angle above the horizon from a scale around the edge.

In the West

At the same time, astronomy was flourishing in Central America, a part of the world unknown to either European, Indian, or Arab astronomers. There, the Mayan civilization was at its peak. Mayan astronomers were meticulous observers who left detailed records in manuscripts and carved in stone. They kept particularly accurate records of the movements of Venus, by which they checked their calendar. They could also predict when eclipses would take place.

European Astronomy Reborn

By the 15th century, a general revival of learning was underway in Europe. This period became known as the Renaissance. People began developing new ideas and challenging age-old beliefs. Among them was the Polish astronomer Nicolaus Copernicus.

Copernicus questioned Ptolemy's Earth-centered view of the universe. He realized that what seemed to be odd movements of the planets in the sky could be better explained if Earth circled the Sun. Thus, the old idea of a sun-centered, or solar, system was reborn.

Copernicus did not publish his ideas until he lay on his deathbed in 1543. He knew that they would upset the accepted view of the universe held by the Catholic Church, which taught that Earth was the center of the Universe.

Nicolaus Copernicus

Left: An armillary sphere was an early astronomical device for representing "great circles" in the heavens, such as the meridian (north-south circle) and ecliptic—the path the Sun seems to take through the heavens during the year.

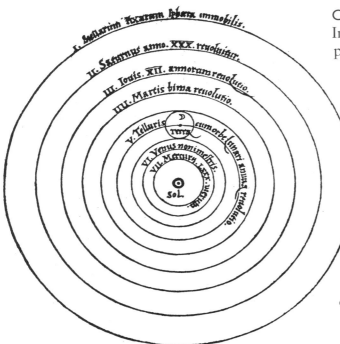

Convincing Evidence

In the years that followed, the Church did punish people who agreed with Copernicus's ideas about the solar system. Eventually astronomers provided convincing evidence that it was right.

One was a German astronomer named Johannes Kepler. He used the very accurate observations made by the Danish astronomer Tycho Brahe to work out exactly how the planets moved through the sky. He proved that their motions could be explained precisely if they traveled around the Sun in oval, or elliptical orbits. He published this finding in 1609 as the first of his celebrated laws of planetary motion.

Above: A sketch by Copernicus showing his solar system, centered on the Sun (Sol). Earth (Terra) becomes just another planet.

Right: Tycho Brahe's famous observatory Uraniborg ("Castle of the Heavens") on the island of Hven, Denmark, built in 1576. It boasted the finest instruments of the time.

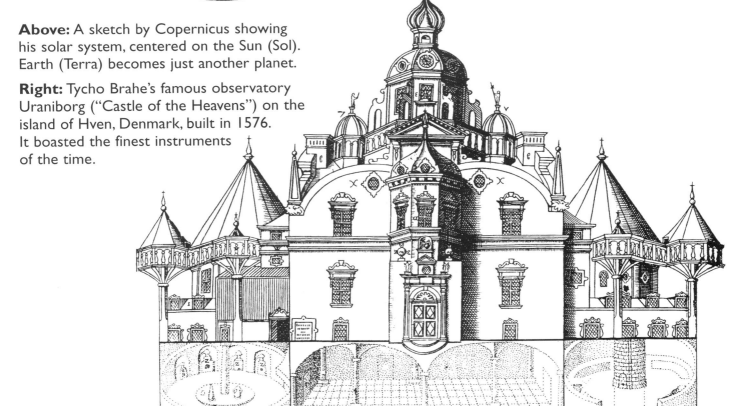

The New Look of the Universe

In 1609, an Italian astronomer named Galilei, known to history as Galileo, ushered in a new revolution in astronomy. He built himself a telescope and turned it on the heavens. He saw things no one had seen before, including the phases, or varying shapes of Venus, and four large moons circling round Jupiter. These observations provided clear evidence of a solar system.

Galileo was a scientific genius. Among other things, he carried out experiments with falling bodies. He died in 1642, the same year that another genius was born in England, whose theories about falling bodies led to the formation of the laws of gravity. His name was Isaac Newton, who started thinking about gravity after seeing apples fall from a tree in 1666. Newton's laws of gravity explained why the Moon and the planets move as they do.

Newton worked and experimented in many other branches of science, particularly optics (the study of light). In about 1668 he built a new kind of telescope that used mirrors to collect and focus light. It provided a clearer image than the lens-type, or refracting, telescope, built by Galileo. Most astronomers today use mirror-type, or reflecting, telescopes.

Finding New Worlds

Astronomers began building bigger and bigger telescopes, both refracting and reflecting, so that they could look deeper into the universe. In 1781 in England, a musician-turned astronomer named William Herschel startled the world of astronomy by finding a new planet.

William Herschel

Called Uranus, it was the first planet discovered in centuries. It proved to be twice as far away as Saturn, the most distant planet previously known. Astronomers then began searching for other new planets. They discovered some mini-planets, or asteroids, in the early 19th century, and another large planet, Neptune, in 1846. The last of the nine planets, Pluto, was not discovered until 1930.

Left: A portrait of Galileo, used as a frontispiece for one of his books.

The Expanding Universe

By this time, astronomers were finding that the universe was much bigger and more complicated than suspected. Large telescopes showed that some of the misty patches, or nebulas, in the night sky had a spiral structure. In the 1920's, U.S. astronomer Edwin Hubble used the 100-inch Hooker telescope to spot stars in some nebulas. The nebulas proved to be separate galaxies far beyond our own.

Observations of the galaxies showed that they were rushing headlong away from one another. This led to the idea that the universe was growing bigger, or expanding, and that it had originated billions of years ago, in a single event, the so-called Big Bang.

In the 1930s, an American engineer named Karl Jansky detected radio waves coming from the heavens. This led to the creation of a new branch of astronomy, known as radio astronomy. Radio astronomy has since become one of the most exciting branches of astronomy, leading to the discovery of strange bodies, such as quasars and pulsars.

In the early 1940s, during World War II, German scientists built powerful V2 rockets as devastating weapons. By the late 1950s rockets had become powerful enough to launch objects into space, beginning with the Russian satellite Sputnik 1 in 1957.

In a short time, astronomers began to launch telescopes and other instruments into space on satellites and probes. These robot explorers have revealed a universe that is ever more beautiful, complex, and mysterious.

Above: The Lovell telescope at Jodrell Bank radio observatory, near Manchester, England. With a dish diameter of 250 feet (76 meters), it is one of the largest fully steerable radio telescopes in the world.

Above: Space probes like *Mariner 9* have revolutionized our study of the solar system, transmitting images and other data from the planets and their moons.

THE CONSTELLATIONS

The stars shine down on us from the great dark dome of the heavens. The brightest ones glow like beacons and guide us around the night sky. Long ago, humans thought they detected patterns in the stars. They gave these shapes and patterns the names by which they are still known today—the constellations.

The ancient astronomers saw virtually the same constellations as we see today. Even over thousands of years, the stars of the constellations barely change position.

People began naming the constellations more than 5,000 years ago. They named them after the figures, shapes, and patterns they thought they saw—a lion here, a swan there.

Astronomers often use Latin names for the constellations, so lion becomes the constellation Leo, and the swan becomes Cygnus.

There are interesting stories about most of the constellations. The Greeks named nearly 50 of them, often relating them to their myths, or traditional stories. Birds, fish, sea monsters, even everyday objects found their way into the sky, each with a tale to tell.

Some of the brightest stars in the constellations have their own names. For example, the brightest star in the whole heavens is in the constellation Canis Major (Great Dog). It is named Sirius and is more popularly called the Dog Star.

The third-brightest star in the heavens is in the constellation Centaurus (Centaur). It is usually called Alpha Centauri. Astronomers use this kind of name all the time, using a Greek letter followed by the constellation name. Alpha is the first letter in the Greek alphabet, which tells us that Alpha Centauri is the brightest star in Centaurus. Beta Centauri is the second-brightest star, and so on.

Left: The constellation Taurus is depicted as the head of a charging bull. The bright reddish star Aldebaran marks the bull's eye.

Right: Globe-shaped masses of stars like this are found in many of the constellations. Called globular clusters, they can contain hundreds of thousands of stars packed closely together.

In the Same Direction

The stars in the constellations look as if they are grouped quite close together in space. But they are actually immense distances from one another. The stars in a constellation only look close together because they happen to lie in the same direction in space when we view them from Earth.

For example, the nearest star to us in the constellation Orion is about 300 light years away from Earth. But the bright star Betelgeuse is over 600 light years away, and Rigel is over 800 light years away.

All Change

The constellations seem as if they never change. Their stars always seem to stay in the same positions, which is why we see the same constellations as the ancient Babylonians did thousands of years ago.

Astronomers tell us that the constellations are changing all the time—but so little and so slowly that our eyes cannot detect the change. By studying light from the stars, astronomers know that they are all traveling very fast indeed. The reason we cannot see them move is because they are so very far away—trillions upon trillions of miles.

Below: The constellation Orion, as depicted by ancient astronomers. He is a mighty hunter, seen here kneeling, with a raised club in his right hand poised to strike a blow.

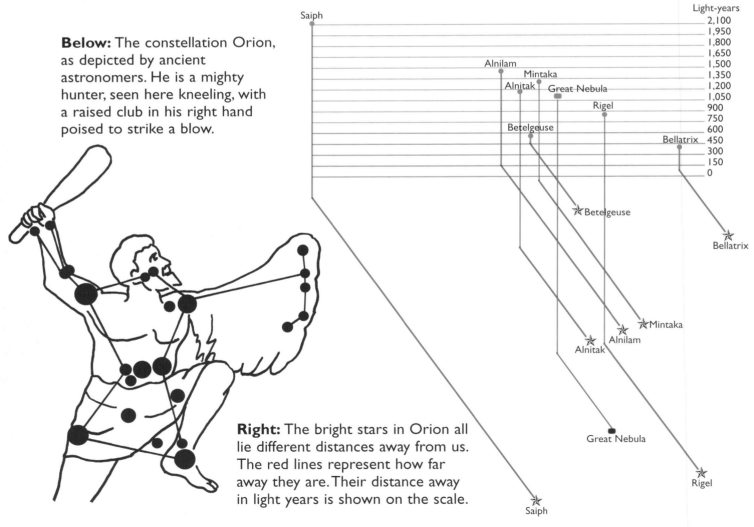

Right: The bright stars in Orion all lie different distances away from us. The red lines represent how far away they are. Their distance away in light years is shown on the scale.

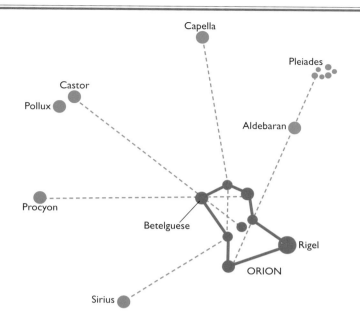

Above: Orion is an excellent signpost to other stars, including the brightest star, Sirius.

But if we were able to return to Earth millions of years from now, it would appear to us that the stars have moved. The constellations would no longer appear as the same patterns because the stars are all moving in different directions.

Guiding the Way

The constellations can help us find our way around the heavens, serving as signposts to other constellations, individual stars, and other features.

In the Northern Hemisphere, the Big Dipper is a good signpost. A line through the two stars at the end of the dipper points to the Pole Star, Polaris. Polaris is also called the North Star because it is located in the heavens directly above the North Pole. When you find it you know you are looking north. Sailors have used the Pole Star to navigate at sea for centuries.

Right: A dark celestial sphere appears to surround Earth. The stars seem to be stuck on the inside of the sphere.

Stargazers in both the Northern and Southern Hemisphere can use another unmistakable constellation Orion as a guide. As the illustration shows, it can be used to locate a host of stars in other constellations.

The Celestial Sphere

Ancient astronomers believed that the stars were stuck on the inside of a great round ball that surrounded Earth. They called this ball the celestial, or heavenly, sphere.

We still use the idea of a celestial sphere even though we know that it does not actually exist. We imagine the sphere to be divided into two halves. One half covers the Northern Hemisphere of the world, and the other half the Southern Hemisphere. They meet along an imaginary line, which we call the celestial equator. It lies directly over the Earth's Equator.

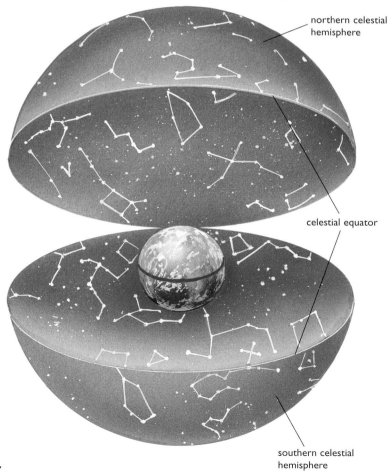

northern celestial hemisphere

celestial equator

southern celestial hemisphere

Northern Constellations

Constellations of the northern celestial hemisphere.

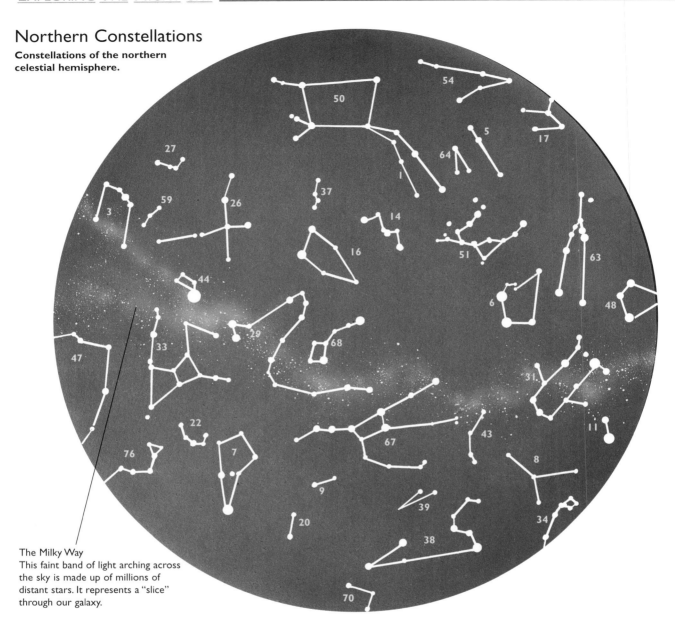

The Milky Way
This faint band of light arching across the sky is made up of millions of distant stars. It represents a "slice" through our galaxy.

1 Andromeda	13 Carina (Keel)	25 Crux (Southern Cross)
2 Aquarius (Water-Bearer)	14 Cassiopeia	26 Cygnus (Swan)
3 Aquila (Eagle)	15 Centaurus (Centaur)	27 Delphinus (Dolphin)
4 Ara (Altar)	16 Cepheus	28 Dorado (Swordfish)
5 Aries (Ram)	17 Cetus (Whale)	29 Draco (Dragon)
6 Auriga (Charioteer)	18 Chamaeleon (Chameleon)	30 Eridanus
7 Boötes (Herdsman)	19 Columba (Dove)	31 Gemini (Twins)
8 Cancer (Crab)	20 Coma Berenices (Berenice's Hair)	32 Grus (Crane)
9 Canes Venatici (Hunting Dogs)	21 Corona Australis (Southern Crown)	33 Hercules
10 Canis Major (Great Dog)	22 Corona Borealis (Northern Crown)	34 Hydra (Water Snake)
11 Canis Minor (Little Dog)	23 Corvus (Crow)	35 Hydrus (Little Snake)
12 Capricornus (Sea Goat)	24 Crater (Cup)	36 Indus (Indian)

Southern Constellations

Constellations of the southern celestial hemisphere.

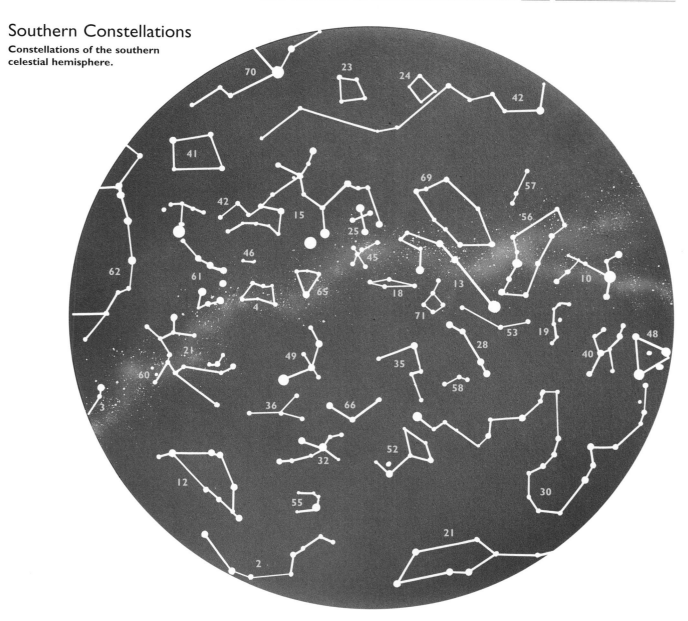

37 Lacerta (Lizard)	49 Pavo (Peacock)	61 Scorpius (Scorpion)
38 Leo (Lion)	50 Pegasus (Flying Horse)	62 Serpens (Serpent)
39 Leo Minor (Little Lion)40	51 Perseus	63 Taurus (Bull)
Lepus (Hare)	52 Phoenix (Phoenix)	64 Triangulum (Triangle)
41 Libra (Scales)	53 Pictor (Painter)	65 Triangulum Australe (Southern Triangle)
42 Lupus (Wolf)	54 Pisces (Fishes)	66 Tucana (Toucan)
43 Lynx (Lynx)	55 Piscis Austrinus (Southern Fish)	67 Ursa Major (Great Bear)
44 Lyra (Lyre)	56 Puppis (Poop)	68 Ursa Minor (Little Bear)
45 Musca (Fly)	57 Pyxis (Compass)	69 Vela (Sails)
46 Norma (Rule)	58 Reticulum (Net)	70 Virgo (Virgin)
47 Ophiuchus (Serpent-Bearer)	59 Sagitta (Arrow)	71 Volans (Flying Fish)
48 Orion	60 Sagittarius (Archer)	

The Constellations You See

Even if you spend every night of the year stargazing, you will never be able to see all 88 constellations. Because Earth is round, part of the sky is always hidden from view.

For example, if you live in Vermont, the Little Dipper and the Pole Star, Polaris, will be old friends. But you will never see Crux, the famous Southern Cross, which lies "down under" in the far south of the heavens. On the other hand, stargazers in South Australia will be familiar with Crux, but will never see the Little Dipper.

Looking at Latitude

In general, over the course of a year an observer in the Northern Hemisphere will be able to see all the constellations of the northern celestial hemisphere and some of those of the southern. Similarly, an observer in the Southern Hemisphere will be able to see all the constellations of the southern celestial hemisphere and some of those of the northern.

Exactly which constellations stargazers will see depends on their latitude, or how far away they are away from Earth's Equator.

Below: Because Earth is round, observers in different parts of the world see different views of the heavens.

Below: Going to a planetarium is a good way of learning about the stars and other heavenly bodies. In a planetarium, a special projector throws images of the night sky on a domed ceiling.

The Whirling Heavens

When you stargaze for any length of time, you will notice that the constellations seem to slowly change positions, moving across the sky from east to west. New stars seem to continually rise above the horizon in the east, while others set beneath the horizon in the west. The entire celestial sphere seems to spin around, which is what the ancient astronomers believed. But they were wrong.

It is Earth that spins around in space from west to east, and this makes the heavens seem to spin around us in the opposite direction.

Star Maps and Planisphere

Because Earth moves, which constellations you see and where they are in the sky depends on the time of the night at which you are viewing.

Right: A planisphere has a movable disc on top, which rotates over a map of the heavens. When you line up the observing time (on the movable disc) with the date (on the base), a view of the night sky at that time and date appears in the transparent window.

A very useful tool that all stargazers should take with them is a planisphere. This device shows the constellations visible in the sky at any time of the night on every night of the year. Because our view of the heavens depends on how far north or south of the Equator we are, different planispheres are made for different latitudes.

Planisphere
shows the principal stars visible
for every hour in the year
for Latitude 42°N
USA • Southern Europe
• Northern Japan

Left: Circular star trails. You get a picture like this when you point your camera at the Pole Star and leave the camera shutter open for an hour or more. The stars make circular trails because Earth is spinning beneath them.

THE CHANGING HEAVENS

The night sky does not change only during the course of the night. It also changes gradually during the year. Month by month, different constellations sweep into view while others disappear, making the heavens in each season distinctly different.

Look south in the sky in the evening around the turn of the New Year and you will see the brilliant constellation Orion. Look in the same direction at the same time of night three months later and you will see the unmistakable shape of Leo (Lion). Orion will have all but disappeared over the western horizon. As the months go by, Leo moves on and is replaced by other constellations.

The constellations seem to come and go like this because Earth circles in orbit around the Sun during the year. Every month, Earth travels a little further in its orbit. This means that each night we look out onto a slightly different part of the heavens—of the so-called celestial sphere. After several months, our view is of quite a different part of the heavens. Therefore we see different constellations.
Because Earth always completes its orbit of the Sun in one year, each year we can see the same constellations in the same place in the sky at the same time of the year. In the next pages, we look at the constellations that appear in the heavens season by

season—in spring, summer, fall, and winter. The main maps show the stars visible at about 10 P.M. to stargazers in the United States and other countries in the Northern Hemisphere.

The sky views shown are not exactly what all stargazers will see. What you will see depends on your latitude, or how far you are away from the equator. If you live in the Great Lakes region, for example, you will be able to see a little farther north, while someone who lives in Florida will be able to see a little farther south.

Stargazers in the Southern Hemisphere of the world have different views of the night sky. The constellations familiar to northern stargazers appear upside-down to them. In addition, the seasons are different as well. Spring in the northern hemisphere is fall in the southern hemisphere, winter in the north is summer in the south, and so on.

Opposite: The dazzling Pleiades star cluster, also called the Seven Sisters. It is one of the highlights of the constellation Taurus.

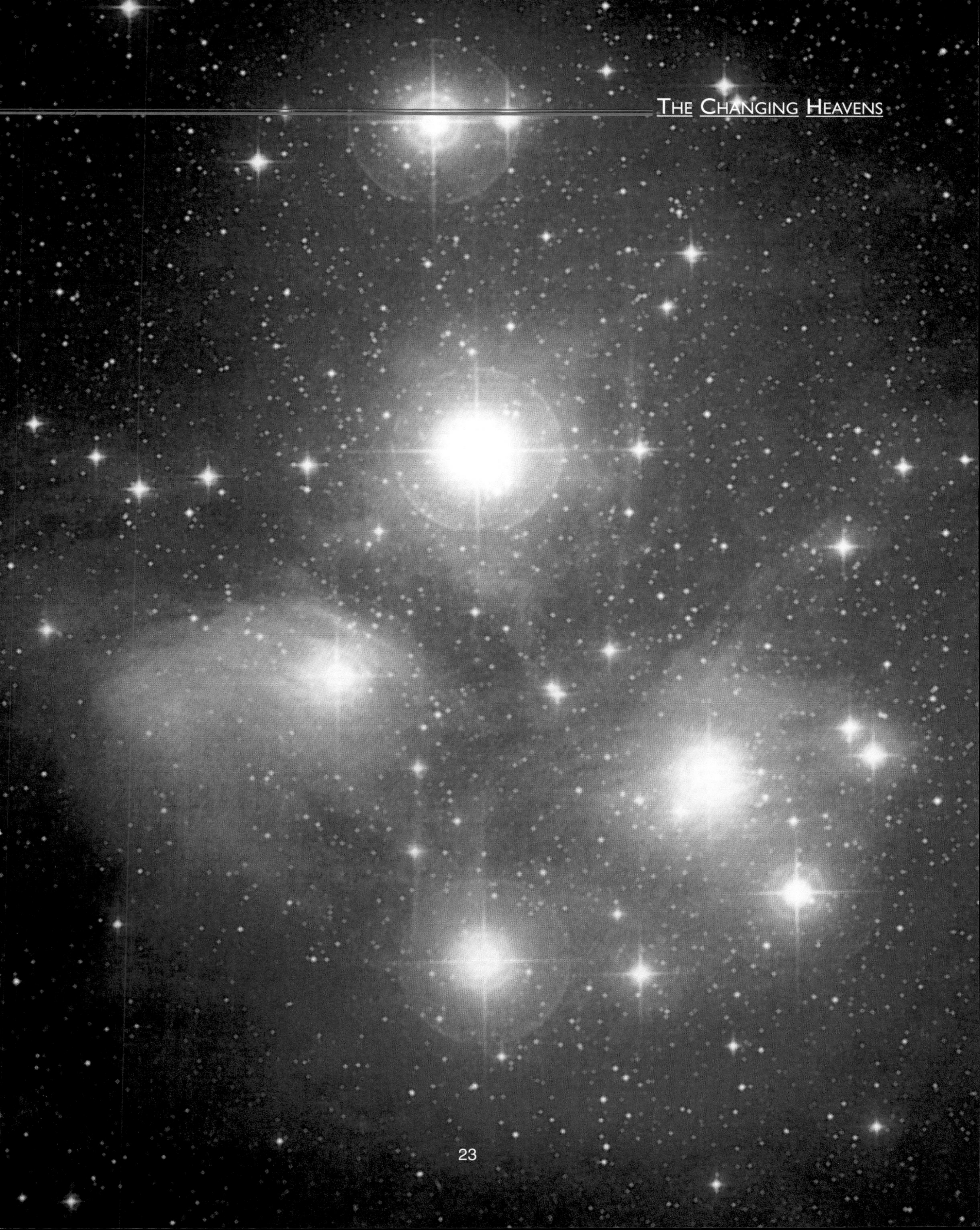

Spring Stars

By mid-April, the Big Dipper has reached its highest point in the heavens and is almost directly above the Pole Star, Polaris. In contrast, Cassiopeia is almost at its lowest point and sits on the northern horizon.

Two bright stars have risen above the horizon in the north-east. They are Deneb in Cygnus (Swan) and Vega in Lyra (Lyre). Deneb is much farther away than Vega but shines brightly because it has the brilliance of 50,000 Suns.

Northern Hemisphere
Looking north

Mid-April sky
at about 10 pm

Northern Hemisphere
Looking south

Mid-April sky
at about 10 pm

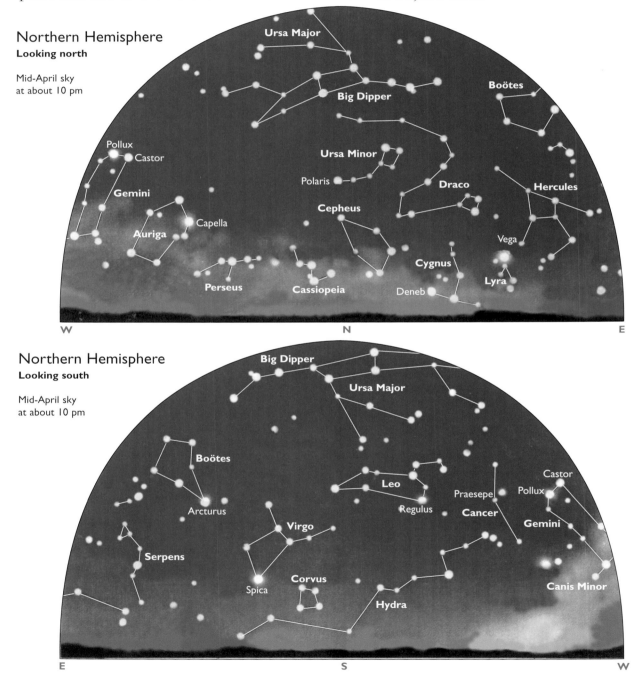

Cygnus lies in the Milky Way, which at this time is located close to the horizon. Viewed through binoculars, the Milky Way is a delight—sprinkled with millions of close-packed stars, clusters, and shining gas clouds.

Looking South

The easiest constellation to recognize is Leo (Lion). Its brightest star, Regulus, and the curve of stars above it form a pattern aptly named the Sickle. To the west are the two brightest stars of Gemini (Twins), Castor and Pollux.

In between Leo and Gemini, there is a little group of stars in Cancer (Crab) that you can see with the naked eye. This cluster is called the Beehive because the scattered stars look like bees buzzing around a hive.

Towards the east, two bright stars shine out of a generally dull part of the sky. One is Arcturus in Boötes (Herdsman), which is the brightest star in the northern hemisphere and the fourth-brightest overall. The other brilliant star is Spica, the leading star in Virgo (Virgin).

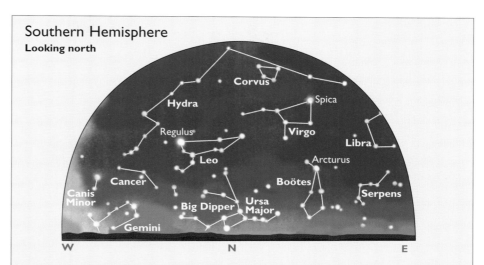

Southern Hemisphere
Looking north

When it is spring in the Northern Hemisphere of the world, it is fall in the Southern Hemisphere. Looking north in the April sky, southern observers see most of the constellations that northern observers see when they look south, but upside-down.

Leo is prominent in the mid-sky. Its brightest star, Regulus, forms a conspicuous triangle with two other bright stars—Arcturus and Spica.

This month southern observers have a rare chance to see the Big Dipper, which appears low down on the northern horizon.

Looking South

The skies are, as ever, dazzling. Crux (Southern Cross) is in the mid-sky almost due south. It is one of the many gems in the bright arc of the Milky Way. The two brightest stars in the whole heavens, Sirius and Canopus, shine like beacons in the south-west.

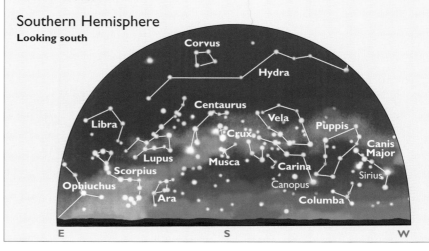

Southern Hemisphere
Looking south

Summer Stars

If you look north at 10 P.M. on an evening in mid-July, the Big Dipper is descending, while Cassiopeia is climbing. Pegasus and Andromeda are rising in the east, bringing into view the misty patch known as the Great Nebula in Andromeda. It is actually a galaxy, the light of which has been traveling toward us for more than 2,000,000 years. It is the most distant heavenly body we can see with our eyes alone. A powerful telescope is needed to see its individual stars.

Northern Hemisphere
Looking north

Mid-July sky
at about 10 pm

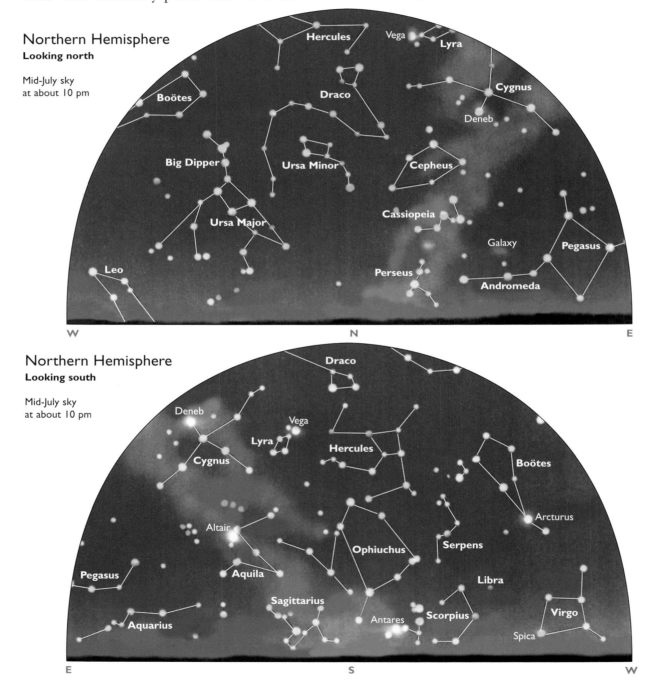

Northern Hemisphere
Looking south

Mid-July sky
at about 10 pm

Looking South

A trio of bright stars hits the eye. They are Altair in Aquila (Eagle), Deneb in Cygnus (Swan), and Vega in Lyra (Lyre). These beacon stars are a distinguishing feature of summer skies and form what is called the Summer Triangle.

Low on the southern horizon, this month observers can glimpse two of the most spectacular constellations of the southern hemisphere. They are Sagittarius (Archer) and Scorpius (Scorpion). Both straddle the Milky Way and are rich in star clouds and clusters. The Milky Way appears dense here; when we look at Sagittarius we are looking into the heart of the galaxy.

In Scorpius, observers should be able to spot the red star Antares, which marks the Scorpion's heart. Stargazers in the southern states may see the curve of bright stars that trace out the animal's deadly stinging tail.

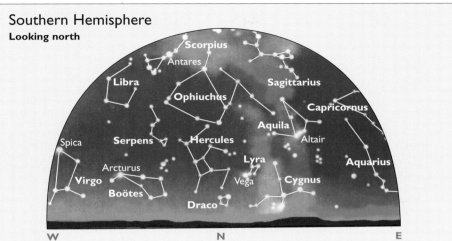

Southern Hemisphere
Looking north

In the Southern Hemisphere, July is a winter month. As the stargazer looks north, three bright stars appear low in the sky. These are the three stars that form the celebrated Summer Triangle in the Northern Hemisphere. They are Deneb, Altair, and Vega. Deneb marks the tail end of the Swan, which here is flying nearly vertically upward through the sky along the Milky Way.

Toward the west appear two constellations very familiar to northern stargazers—Hercules and the kite-shaped Boötes (Herdsman) with its brilliant star Arcturus.

Looking South

The brilliant Milky Way rises almost vertically in the sky. Crux (Southern Cross) is prominent near the horizon, surrounded by the brilliant stars of Centaurus (Centaur). This constellation's brightest star, Alpha Centauri, is one of the nearest stars to us, being only a little over 4 light years away.

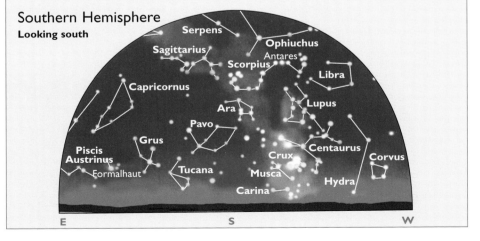

Southern Hemisphere
Looking south

27

Fall Stars

With the coming of fall, the evening skies darken noticeably. The Milky Way is becoming more prominent. In mid-October, it spans the sky from east to west.

As the stargazer looks north, the Big Dipper is reaching its lowest point in its perpetual orbit around the Pole Star, Polaris, and now sits on the horizon. Cassiopeia, by contrast, is now riding high near the top of the arc of the Milky Way.

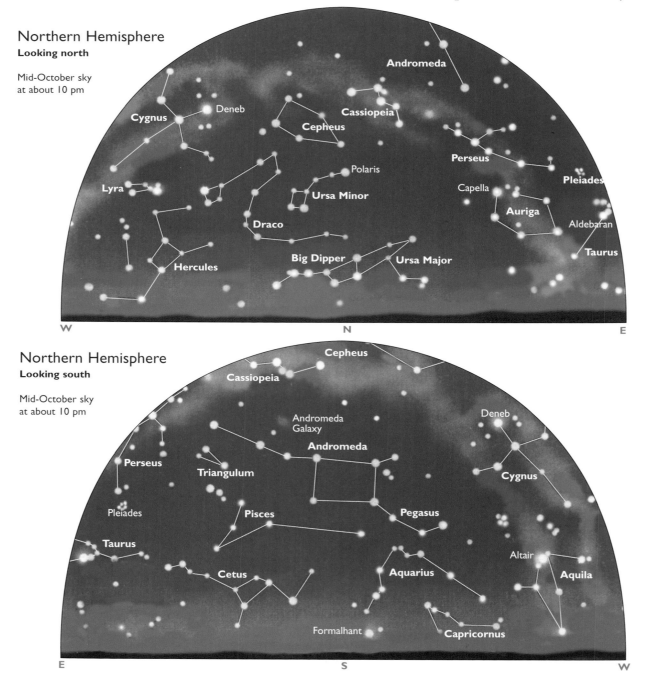

Northern Hemisphere
Looking north

Mid-October sky
at about 10 pm

Northern Hemisphere
Looking south

Mid-October sky
at about 10 pm

Toward the west, Cygnus (Swan) appears in the mid-sky, where its swan shape—long thrusting neck and outstretched wings—can be best appreciated. In the east, Taurus (Bull) has risen, its lead star, Aldebaran, looking extremely red. This star marks the Bull's eye. A little higher in the sky is the best known of all star clusters, the Pleiades, or Seven Sisters.

Looking South

The middle of the sky belongs to Pegasus (Flying Horse). Four of its stars form an unmistakable square. The square provides a useful guide for finding the misty patch that is the Andromeda Galaxy, which lies nearby.

The lower part of the southern sky is occupied by faint and "watery" constellations, such as Pisces (Fishes), Cetus (Whale), and Aquarius (Water-Bearer). The bright star appearing low in the sky near the horizon is Fomalhaut in Piscis Austrinus (Southern Fish).

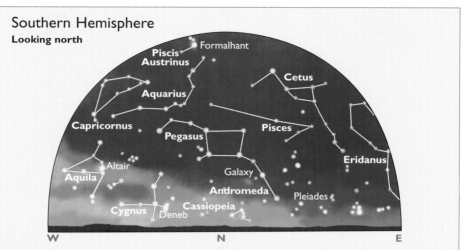

Southern Hemisphere
Looking north

October in the Southern Hemisphere means spring is well on its way. Pegasus and its famous square sits in mid-sky, almost due north. The upper part of the sky is less interesting, filled with faint "watery" constellations.

The Andromeda galaxy and the Pleiades cluster appear quite low in the sky. Toward the west, the bright pair of stars Altair (Eagle) and Deneb (Swan) are also low in the sky and will soon be setting.

Looking South

At this time of the year, the constellations in this part of the sky are faint and difficult to recognize. These include "watery" ones, such as the River Eridanus, and the "flock" of southern birds, such as Phoenix, Grus (Crane), and Pavo (Peacock).

Only close to the horizon does the sky brighten. Bright Rigel and Canopus are rising in the east, while Sagittarius (Archer) and Scorpius (Scorpion) dazzle in the west.

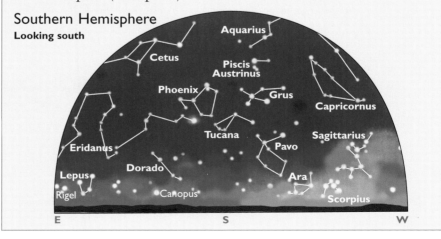

Southern Hemisphere
Looking south

Winter Stars

Winter brings chilly, frosty nights and clearer, darker skies. To the viewer looking north in mid-January, the Milky Way stands vertically. Only the tail end of Cygnus (Swan) is still visible, with Deneb shining brilliantly. Directly above, in mid-sky, is the unmistakable W-shape of Cassiopeia. Higher still, nearly overhead, is Capella, brightest star of Auriga (Charioteer) and the sixth-brightest in the whole heavens.

Northern Hemisphere
Looking north

Mid-January sky
at about 10 pm

Northern Hemisphere
Looking south

Mid-January sky
at about 10 pm

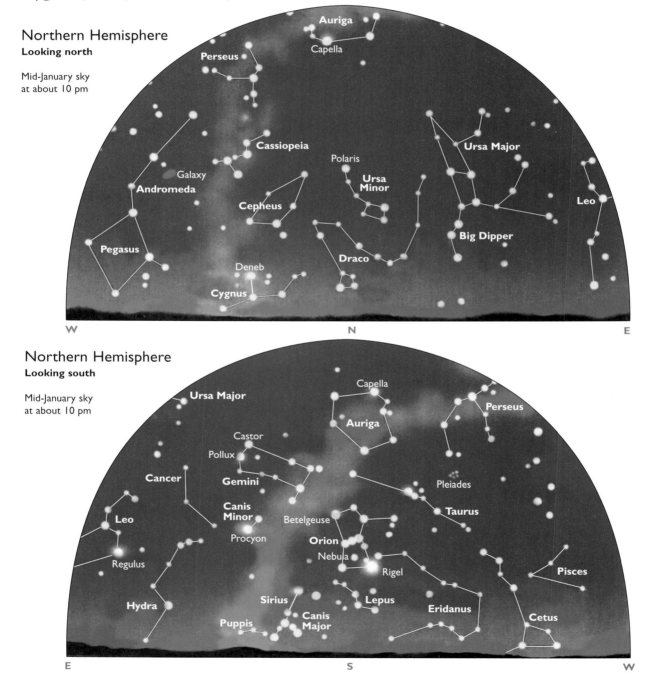

30

Looking South

This month's view of the southern sky is one of the finest of all. It is dominated by the most magnificent of all the constellations, Orion, but also boasts in mid-sky Taurus (Bull) and, across the Milky Way, Gemini (Twins).

Orion features two bright and contrasting stars, orange Betelgeuse and pure white Rigel. It also has a bright nebula, which can be seen with the naked eye under the three stars that form Orion's Belt. This nebula is a vast cloud of glowing gas and dust, where stars are being born all the time.

Orion is not only a brilliant constellation, but also a valuable signpost to other highlights of winter skies. These highlights include the Pleiades star cluster and the brightest star in the heavens, Sirius. Sirius is also called the Dog Star because it is found in the constellation Canis Major (Great Dog).

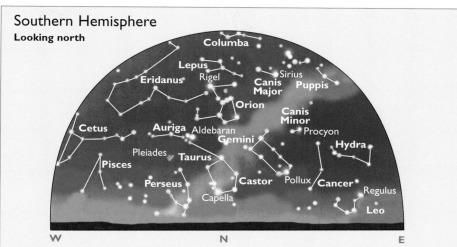

Southern Hemisphere
Looking north

In January, the Southern Hemisphere is in the middle of summer. The nights are short and relatively bright, so they are not ideal for stargazing. Looking north, Orion, Gemini, and Taurus delight the eye.

The brightest stars of these and other constellations form a dazzling ring. They are Rigel, Aldebaran, Capella, Castor, and Pollux, Procyon, and Sirius.

This is a good time to look at the Pleiades, also known as the Seven Sisters. However, you are unlikely to spot all of the seven brightest stars that gave this star cluster its name.

Looking South

Crux (Southern Cross) has just risen above the horizon in a vertical Milky Way. Above it come the brilliant "nautical" constellations of Vela (Sails), Carina (Keel), and Puppis. Carina's brightest star, Canopus, is second in brightness only to Sirius.

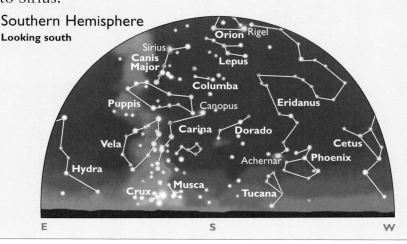

Southern Hemisphere
Looking south

31

During the year, the Sun follows a path around the celestial sphere known as the ecliptic. The planets are always found near the ecliptic in a band called the zodiac.

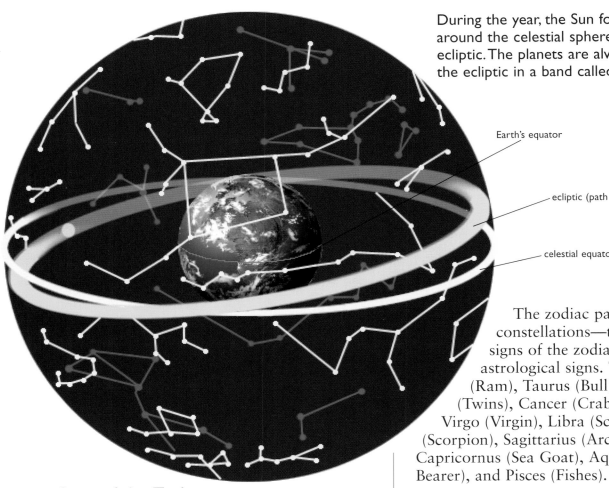

Earth's equator

ecliptic (path of Sun)

celestial equator

The zodiac passes through 12 constellations—the so-called signs of the zodiac, or astrological signs. They are Aries (Ram), Taurus (Bull), Gemini (Twins), Cancer (Crab), Leo (Lion), Virgo (Virgin), Libra (Scales), Scorpius (Scorpion), Sagittarius (Archer) Capricornus (Sea Goat), Aquarius (Water-Bearer), and Pisces (Fishes).

Stars of the Zodiac

Earth is one of the nine planets that circle in space around the Sun. It takes a year to complete this orbit.

But, from Earth, the Sun appears to travel each year in a great circle around the heavens—around the celestial sphere. The path the Sun seems to follow against the background of stars is called the ecliptic.

All the planets circle around the Sun on much the same plane (flat sheet) in space. This means that from Earth, the planets always seem to travel through the heavens close to the path of the Sun. The path it appears that they travel along is referred to as the zodiac.

Something Special

For thousands of years, people have believed that what happened in the heavens could somehow affect their own life. When they saw that the Sun and the planets always appeared to pass through the same constellations, they thought that these constellations might have the ability to affect human affairs.

This belief is known as astrology. Many people still believe in astrology today, but astronomers can find no scientific basis for it.

Your star sign is the constellation the Sun was passing through on the day you were born (see Table).

Astrologers believe that if you are born

under a particular star sign, you will have a certain character. For example, if you were born under Pisces, you will be sensitive and artistic; under Sagittarius, you will be quick-tempered and adventurous.

The positions of the planets within the constellations on the date you were born are very important to astrologers. They use this information to draw up what is called a birth chart. Astrologers include the Sun and the Moon within their list of planets.

Astrologers use the birth chart as a starting point to give you information about yourself and your life. For example, they might use it to explain what has happened to you in the past or to predict what might happen to you in the future.

Right: A typical birth chart drawn up by astrologers. It shows the positions of the planets in the zodiac at the time of a person's birth.

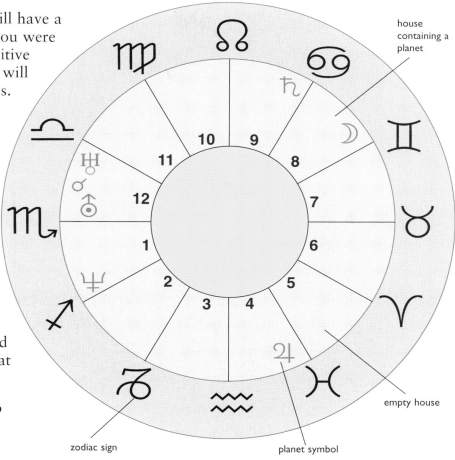

house containing a planet

empty house

zodiac sign

planet symbol

Star Signs

Aries (Ram) March 21–April 20

Taurus (Bull) April 21–May 22

Gemini (Twins) May 23–June 21

Cancer (Crab) June 22–July 22

Leo (Lion) July 23–August 22

Virgo (Virgin) August 23–September 22

Libra (Scales) September 23–October 22

Scorpio (Scorpion) October 23–November 21

Sagittarius (Archer) November 22–December 22

Capricornus (Sea Goat) December 23–January 20

Aquarius (Water-Bearer) January 21–February 19

Pisces (Fishes) February 20–March 20

Above: Twelve constellations are found in the zodiac. The Sun passes through these constellations at the same time every year.

OBSERVING THE HEAVENS

Although we can see a lot of celestial objects in the night sky just with our eyes, we can see much more with the help of binoculars and telescopes. Astronomers use huge telescopes and also send instruments into space to spy on the strange and wonderful bodies that make up our universe.

At the simplest level, all you need to be an astronomer is your eyes. If you stargaze for any length of time, you will soon learn to recognize the patterns of bright stars in the sky—the constellations. You will see how they seem to wheel across the heavens during the night, and how they come and go with the seasons.

You will also notice the very bright stars that often appear to wander among the constellations. These are not stars but planets. They look bigger and brighter than the ordinary stars because they are much closer to earth—millions of miles away rather than trillions of miles.

The biggest and closest body of all, of course, is the Moon. The Moon is responsible for some of the most wonderful sights in nature—eclipses of the Sun—when day turns suddenly into night.

There are other unusual sights in the heavens that can be seen with the eyes alone. Almost every night you can see bright streaks where stars seem to be falling from the sky. Astronomers call these falling stars meteors.

From time to time, large objects with streaming tails appear, blaze through the heavens for a time, and then disappear. These spectacular bodies are comets, icy lumps that have traveled to our skies from the depths of the solar system.

There is, however, a limit to how much you can see with just your eyes. Astronomers therefore use instruments that gather much more light than our eyes can. They are telescopes, a word meaning something like "seeing far."

William Herschel, discoverer of the planet Uranus, built this enormous telescope in 1789, which had a body tube 40 feet (12 meters) long. He used it to discover Saturn's moons Mimas and Enceladus.

34

An observatory dome sits high above the clouds at a mountaintop observatory, where the air is crystal clear. At night the dome opens to expose its powerful telescope to the heavens.

35

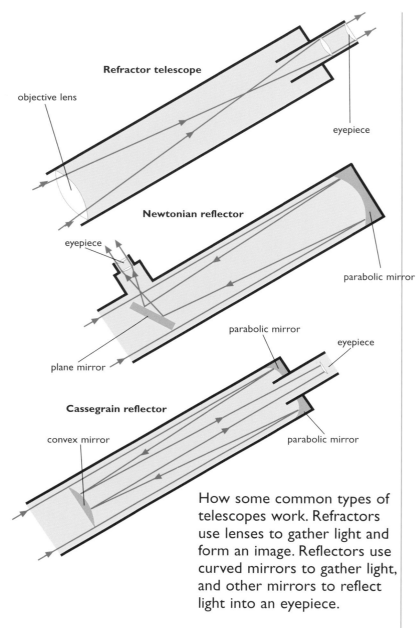

Refractor telescope

objective lens

eyepiece

Newtonian reflector

eyepiece

parabolic mirror

plane mirror

parabolic mirror

eyepiece

Cassegrain reflector

convex mirror

parabolic mirror

How some common types of telescopes work. Refractors use lenses to gather light and form an image. Reflectors use curved mirrors to gather light, and other mirrors to reflect light into an eyepiece.

Looking at Telescopes

The kind of telescope Galileo used to look at the heavens is known as a refractor, or refracting telescope. It is so called because it has glass lenses that refract, or bend light. Many amateur astronomers use refractors, which are easy to build in small sizes and easy to set up and use.

An amateur astronomer uses a small refractor. Such instruments are ideal for beginners.

Two main kinds of lenses are used in a refractor. At the front is the larger one, which is called the objective or object glass. The purpose of this lens is to gather incoming starlight and focus it—form it into a sharp image.

The other main lens is the eyepiece, which the astronomer looks through. The eyepiece is used to look at and magnify the image. It fits in a narrower tube than the objective and can be slid in and out for focusing.

Mirror Telescopes

About 60 years after Galileo had made his first observations, England's Isaac Newton developed a new kind of telescope, which used mirrors to gather light. This kind of instrument is called a reflector, or reflecting telescope, because mirrors reflect light. Most amateur astronomers who use reflectors have instruments called Newtonians, which are based on Newton's original design.

A Newtonian reflector has a shallow, dish-shaped mirror at the base of the telescope body tube. It gathers the incoming starlight and reflects the light to another plane (flat) mirror back up the tube. In turn, this mirror reflects the light into an eyepiece in the side of the tube.

Big Eyes

Generally speaking, the bigger a telescope is, the more it can see of the heavens, revealing even faint objects. The biggest telescopes in the world, the ones used by professional astronomers, are reflectors.

It is difficult to build really big refractors. The lenses have to be supported in the tube of the telescope so that light can pass through them. Big lenses are very heavy and cannot easily be supported in this way. The world's biggest refractor is at the Yerkes Observatory in Wisconsin, which has a 40-inch (1 meter) objective lens.

Because mirrors reflect light from their surface, they can easily be supported from underneath, no matter how big they are. The first giant reflector was the Hale, which has a mirror 200 inches (5 meters) across. Completed in 1948 at Mount Palomar Observatory in California, it is still one of the world's finest instruments.

Today, the most powerful reflectors have even bigger mirrors. They contain not a single flat mirror but one made up of many curved sections. Computers are used to help fit the sections in place to form a perfectly shaped surface. The two Keck telescopes in Hawaii have mirrors 33 feet (10 meters) across, made up of 36 separate sections.

Telescope domes at Mauna Kea Observatory on Hawaii. The photograph captures the moment of totality during the spectacular total eclipse of the Sun on July 11, 1991.

Astronomers at Work

Astronomers go to work at a time—night—when most other people are thinking of going to bed. They carry out their observations and study the results at observatories. The telescopes they use are housed in great domes, which provide protection from the weather. The roofs of the domes open at night to expose the telescopes to the heavens.

Most observatories are sited high on mountain peaks. There, they are above the thickest and dirtiest layers of the atmosphere. Mauna Kea Observatory in Hawaii is one of the highest, located at an altitude of more than 13,500 feet (4,200 meters).

Taking Pictures

These days professional astronomers do not just look through telescopes. Instead they use them as giant cameras and take photographs with them.

There is a very good reason for this. Photographic film can store the light that falls on it. The longer a film is exposed, the more light it will store. Astronomers often expose film in their telescopes for hours at a time. This allows the film to pick up the feeble light from the faintest of objects and make it visible.

When they take such long-exposure photographs, astronomers must allow for the fact that the stars move in relation to Earth. Otherwise the photographs will be

Astronomers generally use black and white film to record images of the heavens. By exposing the film for long periods, they can pick up images of distant objects, such as this spiral galaxy in the constellation Centaurus, which lies millions of light years away.

blurred. The telescopes are mounted on supports so that they move at the same speed and in the same direction as the stars.

Going Electronic

Most telescopes are now guided and controlled with the help of computers. Some are even controlled over long distances through radio links.

Electronics now also plays a vital role in making observations with telescopes. Many telescopes now record images of the heavens on electronic chips instead of photographic film. Called charge-coupled devices, or CCDs, they are similar to the chips used to form the image in videocameras. They are more sensitive to light than film.

Looking at Starlight

The most useful of the many other instruments astronomers use is the spectrograph. They use this instrument to study the faint light from stars in minute detail.

Starlight is like sunlight. It looks white but it is actually made up of a mixture of different colors. We see the colors in sunlight when we pass it through a prism. They form a spectrum. In a similar way a spectrograph splits starlight into a spectrum. By studying dark lines in the spectrum, astronomers can tell all kinds of things about a star, such as its temperature, what it's made of, and how fast it's traveling through space.

Below: The distinctive McMath solar telescope at Kitt Peak National Observatory. Kitt Peak is one of the world's finest observatories, located on a mountain peak near Tucson, in Arizona.

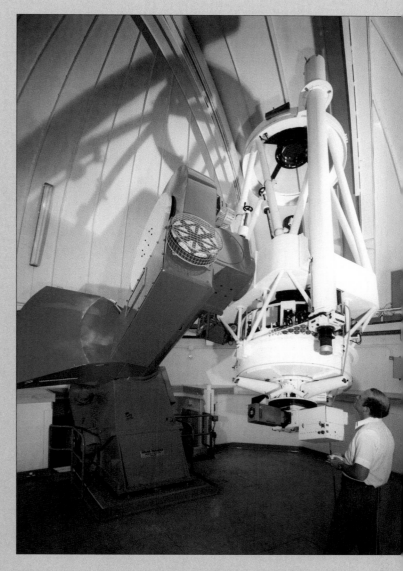

Above: An astronomer works with a 40-inch (1-meter) telescope at the Roque de los Muchachos Observatory in the Canary Islands. Like all modern instruments, it has an open body tube and is computer controlled.

Invisible Astronomy

Most astronomers learn about the heavens by studying the light that stars and galaxies give out. But studying starlight by itself does not give a true picture of what the universe is like. This is because stars give off not only light rays we can see but also many other kinds of rays that are invisible. These rays include gamma rays, X-rays, and radio waves.

Only by looking at all the rays stars give out—visible and invisible—can astronomers build up a complete picture of what the universe is like. But there is a problem. Most invisible rays from space are partly or completely blocked by Earth's atmosphere. Only radio waves get through easily.

The Radio Window

The person who discovered this was a communications engineer named Karl

Jansky, who worked at the Bell Telephone Laboratories in Holmdel, New Jersey. In 1931, he was investigating the hissing noises, or interference, that plagued long-distance communication by short-wave radio. He built a radio receiver from an antenna that circled round a track on the wheels from on old Model T Ford.

Jansky traced much of the interference to local sources or to the atmosphere. But some interference remained, no matter where he pointed the antenna. He suddenly realized that the interference was coming from the sky. The heavens were beaming down radio waves on the Earth.

Jansky's discovery paved the way for a whole new branch of astronomy. Radio astronomy is now one of the most exciting branches of astronomy. It has led to the discovery of intriguing heavenly bodies such as quasars, pulsars, and immensely energetic radio galaxies.

Radio Telescopes

Astronomers gather the radio waves that come from the heavens with radio telescopes. They are quite unlike ordinary light telescopes. Most take the form of huge metal dishes, with an antenna in the center.

The dish has to be huge to pick up the heavenly radio signals, which are very faint. It focuses the signals on the antenna, which then feeds them to a very sensitive radio receiver. Using computers, astronomers can then process the signals and display them as radio "pictures."

The largest dish radio telescope is built in a natural mountain valley on the Caribbean island of Puerto Rico. It measures 1,000 feet (305 meters) across. Some radio telescopes have several smaller dishes that work together to form a much bigger collecting area. A notable example of this type of radio telescope is the Very Large Array near Socorro, New Mexico. It uses 27 movable dishes, each 82 feet (25 meters) across.

Above: The Very Large Array radio telescope at Socorro, New Mexico. Its 27 dishes can be arranged in different patterns to concentrate incoming radio waves.

Left: This steerable radio telescope collects radio waves with its huge dish, which focuses them on the antenna above. The radio signals are processed by computer into false-color images.

Right: The Arecibo radio telescope is fixed and scans the heavens as the Earth rotates.

Far right: Spacewalking astronauts visit the Hubble Space Telescope regularly to make repairs and update instruments.

Right: This Hubble picture shows delicate filaments of glowing gas around the stars of the Pleiades star cluster.

Space Astronomy

To study the other invisible rays given off by stars, astronomers use space technology. They send their telescopes and other instruments into space on spacecraft that travel well above Earth's atmosphere.

Some spacecraft are satellites, which circle Earth repeatedly in orbit. Others are probes, which escape from Earth completely and travel deep into the solar system to visit planets and their moons, asteroids, and comets.

Astronomy Satellites

Satellites have been launched to study all the invisible radiation given off by stars—gamma rays, X-rays, ultraviolet rays, infrared rays, and microwaves. The results they have sent back have added greatly to our knowledge of the universe and how it began and developed.

The most outstanding astronomy satellite looks at the universe in visible light. It is the Hubble Space Telescope (HST), launched

from the space shuttle orbiter Discovery in April 1990.

The HST was expected to look much farther into space than ever before and show stars and galaxies in fantastic detail. But at first, the pictures it sent back were not much better than the best Earth-based telescopes. The curve of its light-gathering mirror was slightly off because of a problem with the way it had been made.

However, a daring space mission in December 1993 repaired the HST, and it began beaming the most fantastic pictures back to Earth. They showed stars being born in spectacular clouds; solar systems in the making; stars puffing off great masses of gas as they die; the remains of stars that have blasted themselves apart; and huge donuts of glowing matter that could hide the most awesome of heavenly objects—black holes.

Space Probes

Space probes have been flying into deep space since the 1960s. They have visited seven of the eight planets besides Earth. Only the most distant planet, icy Pluto, has not yet been explored from space.

The planets and the other heavenly targeted by these probes are extremely far away. Probes take months to reach even the closest planets, Venus and Mars. They take years to reach the others. Probes take so long because for most of the journey time they coast, or travel without power. It would be impossible to provide them with enough fuel to power them all the way.

Sometimes, to reduce the time of their journey, probes loop round other planets and use their gravity to increase speed. This technique is called gravity-assist. It was used by the Voyager probes on their spectacular missions to Jupiter, Saturn, and Uranus, Galileo also used gravity-assist to reach Jupiter, as did Cassini to reach Saturn.

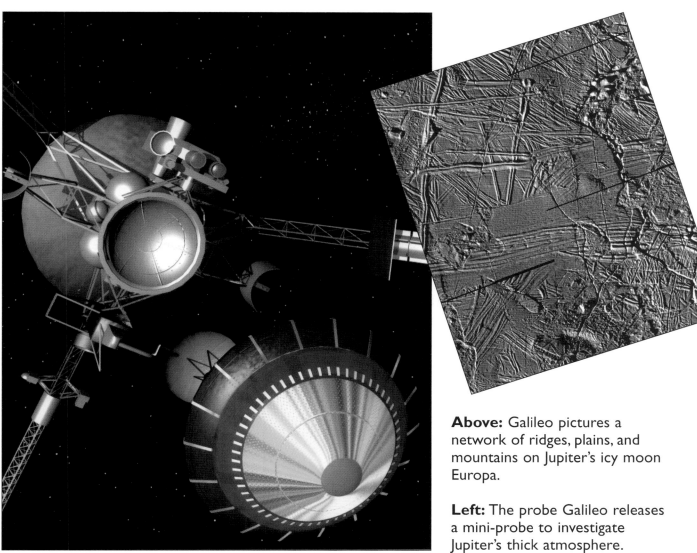

Above: Galileo pictures a network of ridges, plains, and mountains on Jupiter's icy moon Europa.

Left: The probe Galileo releases a mini-probe to investigate Jupiter's thick atmosphere.

Glossary

ASTEROIDS Small lumps of rock or metal that circle the Sun. Most circle in a broad band (the asteroid belt) between the orbits of Mars and Jupiter.

ASTROLOGY A belief that people's characters and everyday lives are somehow affected by the stars and planets.

ASTRONOMY The scientific study of the heavens and the heavenly bodies.

ATMOSPHERE The layer of gases around Earth or another heavenly body.

BIG BANG A fantastic explosion that astronomers think created the Universe about 15 billion years ago.

BLACK HOLE A region of space with enormous gravity; not even light can escape from it.

CALENDAR A way of recording and measuring time. Our calendars are based on the natural divisions of time—the day and the year.

CELESTIAL SPHERE An imaginary dark globe that appears to surround Earth. The stars seem to be fixed to the inside of the sphere.

CLUSTER A group of stars or galaxies. *See also* GLOBULAR CLUSTER.

CONSTELLATION A group of bright stars appearing in the same direction in the sky.

COMET A small icy lump that gives off clouds of gas and dust when it gets near the Sun.

CONSTELLATION A group of bright stars appearing in the same area in the sky.

COSMOS Another word for the universe.

ECLIPSE When one heavenly body passes in front of another and blots out its light. An eclipse of the Sun, or a solar eclipse, takes place when the Moon passes in front of the Sun as we view it from Earth.

EXPANDING UNIVERSE The idea that the Universe is expanding, or getting bigger.

FALLING STAR A popular name for a meteor.

GALAXY A "star island" in space. Our own galaxy is called the Milky Way.

GLOBULAR CLUSTER A globe-shaped group containing hundreds of thousands of stars.

GRAVITY The pull, or force of attraction, that every body has because of its mass.

HEAVENS The night sky; the heavenly bodies are the objects we see in the night sky.

HORIZON The circle around an observer where the land appears to meet the sky.

LATITUDE Of a place; how far it is away from Earth's Equator. It is measured in degrees.

LIGHT-YEAR A unit astronomers use for measuring distances in space. It is the distance light travels in a year—about 6 trillion miles (10 trillion kilometers).

LUNAR To do with the Moon.

NAKED EYE "With the naked eye" means using just the eyes.

NORTHERN HEMISPHERE The half of the world north of the Equator. The northern celestial hemisphere is the part of the sky above the Northern Hemisphere.

MAGNITUDE A measure of a star's brightness.

MILKY WAY A faint band of light seen in the night sky. Our galaxy is also called the Milky Way.

METEOR A streak of light produced when a meteoroid burns up in Earth's atmosphere.

MOON The common name for a satellite.

MEBULA A cloud of gas and dust in space.

OBSERVATORY A place where astronomers work.

ORBIT The path in space one body follows when it circles around another, such as the Moon's orbit around Earth.

PLANET One of nine bodies that circle around the Sun; or more generally, a large body that circles around a star.

PLANISPHERE A circular device for showing the night sky on any night of the year.

POLE STAR Also called North Star; the star that is located in the sky almost directly above Earth's North Pole. Astronomers call it Polaris.

PROBE A spacecraft sent to explore other heavenly bodies, such as planets, moons, asteroids, and comets.

PULSAR A rapidly spinning tiny star, which flashes pulses of light or other radiation toward us.

QUASAR A body that looks like a star but is much farther away than the stars and is as bright as hundreds of galaxies.

RADIATION RAYS The heavenly bodies give off energy as many different kinds of radiation—as light rays, infrared rays, gamma rays, X-rays, ultraviolet rays, microwaves, and radio waves.

RADIO TELESCOPE A telescope designed to gather radio waves from the heavens.

REFLECTOR A reflecting telescope; one that uses mirrors to gather light from the heavens.

REFRACTOR A refracting telescope; one that uses lenses to gather light from the heavens.

SATELLITE A small body that orbits around a larger one; a moon. Also the usual name for an artificial satellite, an orbiting spacecraft.

SEASONS Periods of the year when the temperature and weather are much the same year after year.

SHOOTING STAR A popular name for a meteor.

SOLAR To do with the Sun.

SOLAR SYSTEM The Sun and the bodies that circle around it, including planets, comets, and asteroids.

SOUTHERN SEMISPHERE The half of the world south of the Equator. The southern celestial hemisphere is the part of the sky above the Southern Hemisphere.

SPACE TELESCOPE An artificial satellite that carries telescopes and other astronomical instruments.

STELLAR To do with the stars.

ZODIAC An imaginary band in the heavens, through which the Sun and planets appear to travel.

Important Dates

3000 BC   Astronomy well established in Middle East

585 BC   Greek astronomer Miletus correctly forecasts an eclipse

150 BC   About this time, Hipparchus draws up a star catalog and introduces magnitude scale of brightness

AD 150   About this time, Ptolemy writes an encyclopedia detailing the scientific and astronomical knowledge of the day

800s   Arab astronomy flourishes

1543   Nicolaus Copernicus advances his idea of a solar system

1576   Tycho Brahe sets up advanced observatory on the isle of Hven

1609   Johannes Kepler publishes his first law of planetary motion. Galileo first observes the heavens in a telescope

1668   Isaac Newton builds a reflecting telescope

1781   William Herschel discovers Uranus

1801   Giovanni Piazzi discovers the first asteroid, Ceres

1917   100-inch Hooker reflector completed at Mt Wilson Observatory

1923   Edwin Hubble proves that galaxies are distant star systems

1931   Karl Jansky detects radio waves coming from the heavens

1948   200-inch Hale reflector completed at Mount Palomar Observatory

1957   Russia's *Sputnik 1* launches the Space Age

1963   Arecibo radio telescope completed

1977   Voyager probes launched to the outer planets

1981   Very Large Array radio telescope completed

1990   Hubble Space Telescope launched

1999   Astronomers sight planets around other stars

2004   Cassini-Huygens probe due to encounter Saturn

Further Reading

Large numbers of books on astronomy and space are available in school and public libraries. Librarians will be happy to help you find them. In addition, publishers display their books on the Internet, and you can key into their websites and search for astronomy books. Alternatively, you can look at the websites of on-line bookshops (such as Amazon.com) and search for books on astronomy and space. Here are just a selection of recently published books for further reading.

Constellations by Paul P. Sipiera, Children's Press, 1997
Eyewitness: Astronomy by Kristen Lippincott, Dorling Kindersley, 2000
Map of the Universe, Smithsonian Institution, 1996
Monthly Star Guide by Ian Ridpath and Wil Tirion, Cambridge, 1999
Night Sky by Gary Mechler, National Audubon Society, 1999
See the Stars by Ken Croswell, Boyds Mills Press, 2000
The Sky at Night by Robin Kerrod, New Burlington Books, 2000
Stargazing by Patrick Moore, Cambridge, 2000
Turn Left at Orion by Guy Consolmagno and Dan M. Davis, Cambridge, 2000
The Young Astronomer's Activity Kit, Dorling Kindersley, 2000

Websites

Astronomy and space are popular topics on the Internet, and there are hundreds of interesting websites—details about the latest eclipse, mission to Mars and SETI (Search for Extraterrestrial Intelligence), and so forth.

A good place to start is by using a Search Engine, and search for space and astronomy. Search engines will display extensive listings of topics, which you can then select. For example, you gain access to a list of topics on the Search Engine Yahoo on astronomy with: **http://yahoo.com/Science/Astronomy**

The lists also includes astronomy clubs. If there is one near you, you may well like to join it. Most clubs have interesting programs, with observing evenings, lectures, and visits to observatories.

NASA has many websites covering all aspects of space science, including exploration of the planets and the universe as a whole. The best place to start is at NASA's home page: **http://www.nasa.gov**

From there you can go to, for example, Space Science, which includes planetary exploration. Or you can go directly to: **http://spacescience.nasa.gov/missions**

Individual missions may also have their own website, such as the Mars Odyssey mission at: **http:/mars.jpl.nasa.gov/Odyssey**

The latest information and images from the Hubble Space Telescope can be reached at: **http:/www.stsci.edu/pubinfo** This site will also direct you to picture highlights since the launch of the Telescope in 1990.

European space science activities can be explored via the home page of the European Space Agency at: **http:/www.esa.int**

Index